A FAMILY for JAMIE

· AN ADOPTION STORY ·

Suzanne Bloom

CLARKSON N. POTTER, INC./PUBLISHERS
NEW YORK

In Jamie's family everybody likes to make
things; towers of blocks, cakes with blue
icing, funny masks, stories at bedtime.

Even before they became Jamie's mommy
and daddy, Molly and Dan built and baked,
planted and painted all sorts of things.
One day it was cookies and birdhouses.

Tasting the batter Dan said, "These cookies need raisins." "What they need," said Molly, "is a little child to stir in the raisins and lick the spoon."

When the cookies were done they went down to the garden and set three birdhouses on the fence posts. "Lucky birds," said Dan. "They will

have chicks to care for and teach
how to fly. That's what I want to do."

"Raise chicks?" asked Molly.

"No," sighed Dan, "children."

Molly and Dan could make almost anything, but they couldn't make a baby. They felt very sad. After thinking about it for some time Molly said, "I have a great idea. Let's see if we can adopt a baby." Dan agreed, "That's the best way for us to make our family grow."

So they went to see Ms. Wilton, the adoption counselor. Her job was to make sure that a child who was to be adopted became part of just the right family. Sometimes when a baby's birth parents know they will not be able to take care of him or her, they also may visit Ms. Wilton and ask her to help them choose a loving family for their baby.

Ms. Wilton asked Molly and Dan many questions. "Do you live in the city or the country? What kind of work do you do? What do you do for fun? Do you have any pets?" After Molly and Dan told Ms. Wilton all about themselves, she said, "It usually takes a long time, but I will try to find a baby who needs a mommy and daddy just like you." Molly and Dan went home to wait and plan.

All winter the snow fell in fat flakes.
Every now and then Molly or Dan
would stop work just to imagine
the fun of sledding or making
snow people with their new child.
Molly thought, "We'll read books
and paint pictures and play games
when the north wind keeps us in."

When spring came they planted
their vegetable garden and hoped
that someday soon they would
have a child who might like to help
pick those early peas. Together
they would carry a basketful back
to the kitchen and eat them
up for supper.

Summer settled, hot and sticky.
"We'll teach our baby to swim.
At night we'll look for lightning bugs
and listen to the thunder," said Dan.
"I wonder if our child will like to go
for walks in the woods like I do?"
Molly asked. "I don't know," Dan
replied. "Everybody likes to
do different things."

Finally in the fall Ms. Wilton called
and asked, "Are you ready for a baby?
A wonderful baby has been born

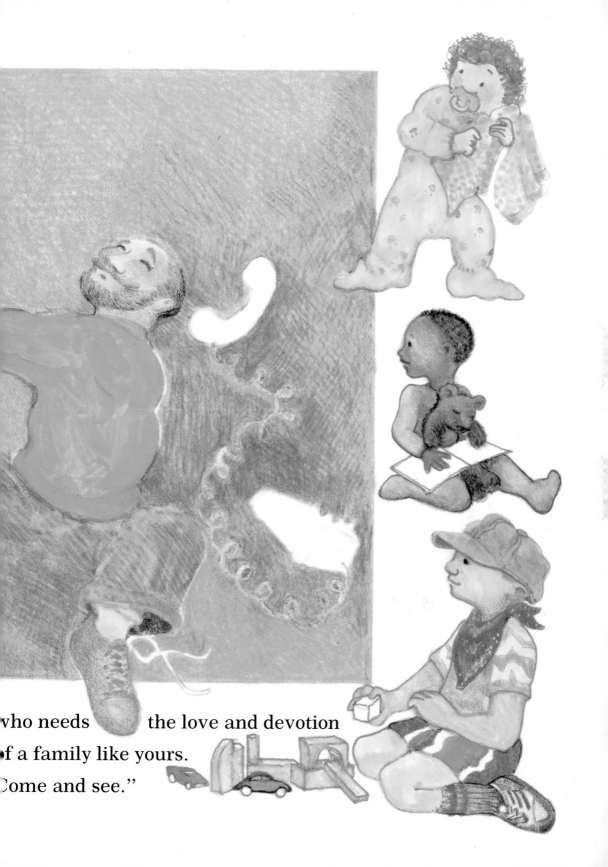

who needs   the love and devotion
of a family like yours.
Come and see.''

They were so excited, they called Grandma and Grandpa, who said, "We know how happy this makes you. We can't wait to see our new grandchild." They called Auntie and Uncle, who said, "Just what you've been hoping for. The crib our children used is ready for your baby. They want to share their baby toys with their new cousin too."

They called their friends, who said, "When we adopted our first daughter we were so busy getting to know each other that we took hardly any photographs. We'll bring some film for your camera. And some diapers."

Molly and Dan smiled as soon as they saw the baby. They hugged and kissed each other and the baby, whom they named Jamie. Then they thanked Ms. Wilton for helping them become Jamie's family and whispered, "Thank you, Jamie, for making us a mommy and daddy." Filled with happiness, Molly, Dan, and Jamie went home to play and learn and grow together.

DEDICATED TO
the birth parents whose
brave and generous choice made the
most wonderful difference
in our lives

Copyright © 1991 by Suzanne Bloom

Text designed by Deb DeStaffan

Published by Clarkson N. Potter, Inc., distributed by Crown Publishers, Inc.,
201 East 50th Street, New York, New York 10022

CLARKSON N. POTTER, POTTER and colophon are trademarks of
Clarkson N. Potter, Inc.

Manufactured in Japan

Library of Congress Cataloging-in-Publication Data
Bloom, Suzanne, 1950–
A family for Jamie: an adoption story by Suzanne Bloom.
p. cm.
Summary: Although Dan and Molly can make cookies and birdhouses, they cannot make
a baby, so they adopt Jamie and share with him their life and love.
[1. Adoption—Fiction.] I. Title.
PZ7.B6234Fam   1990
[E]—dc20   90-42589
CIP
AC
ISBN 0-517-57492-6
0-517-57493-4 (GLB)
10 9 8 7 6 5 4 3 2 1

First Edition